OLIVER'S SWIMMING LESSON

Written and Illustrated by
Teri Runte-Peacock

Xulon Press
2301 Lucien Way #415
Maitland, FL 32751
407.339.4217
www.xulonpress.com

Paperback ISBN-13: 978-1-6628-3200-0

Hard Cover ISBN-13: 978-1-66283-8637

Ebook ISBN-13: 978-1-6628-3201-7

I would like to dedicate this book to my mother, Dianne Runte.
She was an amazing mom and best friend.

_____

I would like to thank my hubby, Paul, for strongly encouraging me to take the plunge to write and illustrate this book. Without his gentle nudges this endeavor probably wouldn't have gotten out of my head and on to paper.

It also wouldn't have gone much further without a lot of encouragement from dear friends and family. Thanks for all the help along the way.

I am so fortunate and blessed!

Meet Oliver. His mom rescued him from a shelter
when he was just a little puppy.
He is a mix of Jack Russel Terrier and Basset Hound.

His mom thinks it's fun to say that he's a Jacket Hound.

He is mostly white with brown freckles all over.
He has brown bouncy ears and a brown patch on one eye.
He also has a half-tail like a Jack Russel and a long body and
short stumpy legs like a Basset Hound.

He is a happy, fun loving dog
that loves running, jumping
and playing around.

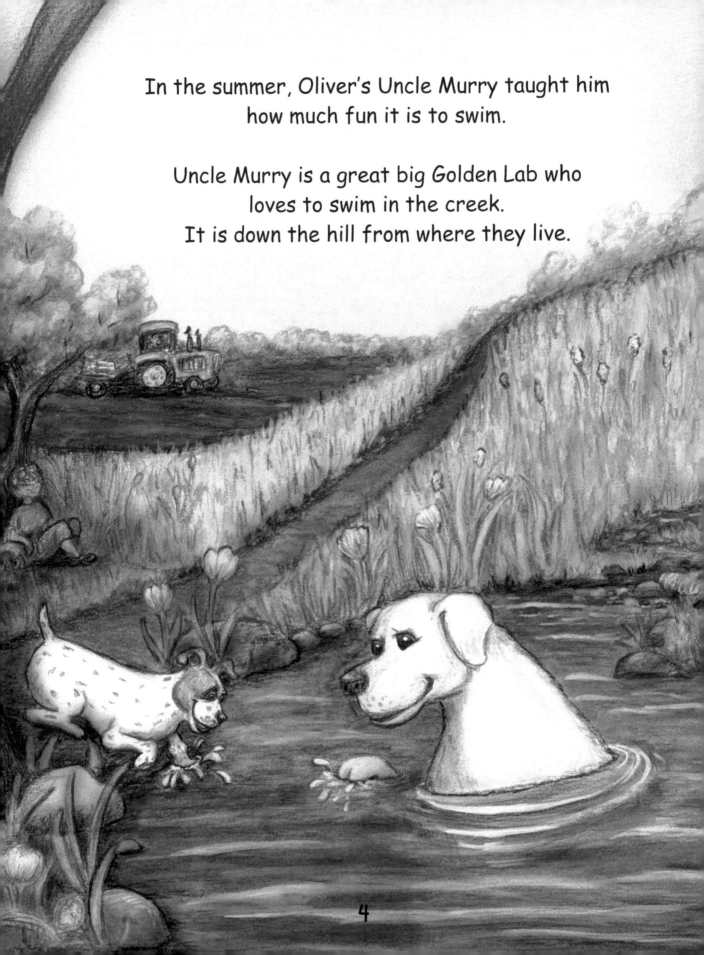

In the summer, Oliver's Uncle Murry taught him
how much fun it is to swim.

Uncle Murry is a great big Golden Lab who
loves to swim in the creek.
It is down the hill from where they live.

They are very lucky to live next
door to each other.
When it is warm Oliver's mom
takes them on walks to the creek
almost every day.

Swimming is one of Oliver's
favorite things to do.

One afternoon while they were at the creek, Oliver saw a frog.
It was sitting on a lily pad enjoying the sunshine.
Oliver thought, "Oh boy! Another friend to play with!"

Oliver plunged into the water!

The frog jumped straight up in the air and ker-sploosh! He landed far away from Oliver and swam away.

That didn't bother Oliver at all because there were a lot of fun things to do besides trying to meet a silly scared frog.

There were sticks to fetch and lots of fun things to smell.

Oliver sniffed right up to a little turtle.
It was so scared of him that it hid right in its shell.

After a few sniffs he left the turtle alone and found
other fun things to investigate.

Oliver always came back to the swimming hole
because that was the most fun. He would splash
around and his mom would throw sticks and he
would swim and swim and swim.

Uncle Murry didn't care for running and jumping
after sticks so he relaxed in the water and
watched energetic Oliver scamper around.

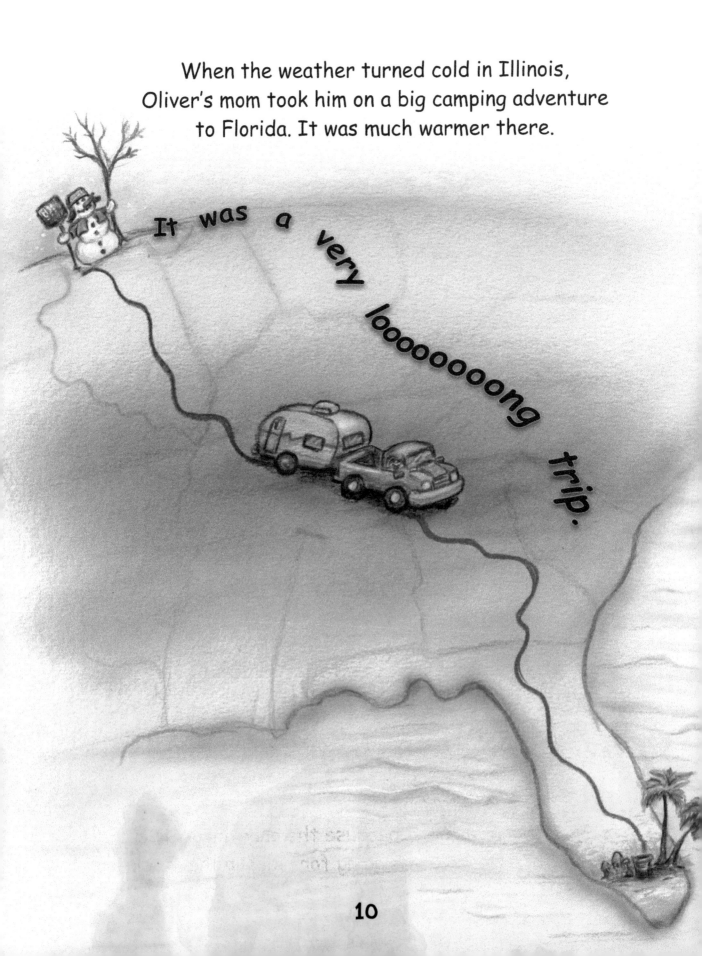

When the weather turned cold in Illinois,
Oliver's mom took him on a big camping adventure
to Florida. It was much warmer there.

It was a very looooooong trip.

A long trip was ok with Oliver because the only thing Oliver liked better than swimming was going for rides in the truck.

One of the first things Oliver and his mom did when they arrived in Florida was visit the ocean. It was the biggest swimming hole Oliver had ever seen! His mom let him swim and splash in the water.

It was definitely different than the creek back home.

It tasted really weird and salty...

...and the waves were really big and a little bit scary.

It was still fun running in the shallow water chasing sea gulls...

...digging holes in the sand and sniffing at shells and starfish...

That is, until one got stuck on his nose.

13

When they arrived at the campground, Oliver got really excited because he saw a canal that looked a lot like the creek back home.

BEWARE of ALLiGATORS

DANGER No Swimming

14

He thought it couldn't get much better than this!
He was going to get to swim all the time and the
water wouldn't taste salty like the ocean.

This was going to be the best place ever!

DOG
WALK →

Oliver made lots of other doggie friends
while they were at the campground.

Two of his best friends are Dewey and Rosie.

Dewey is a short little Wiener dog mix who
wears a bow tie on his collar.

Rosie is an Australian Shepherd mix who has one
blue eye and one brown eye.

Their moms and dads would take them on lots of walks together and they would play and run in the big field that was far away from the canal on the other side of the campground.

Oliver didn't understand why his mom wouldn't let him swim in the canal but he still had fun running and playing with his friends.

One day after it had been raining all morning,
the three dogs went on a walk with their humans.

Oliver was excited because there were water puddles all
around in the field where they played. Water puddles
were almost as good as the canal for fun and splashing.

He showed Dewey and Rosie how much fun it was
to play in the water.

Dewey thought it was all right, but Rosie wasn't having
anything to do with the water. Oliver couldn't understand
why she was afraid of the water. She did like running
and chasing so they still had a lot of fun.

A few days later Oliver met Bart. He is a big Dalmatian with spots all over him. Oliver thought Bart was so cool because his parents let him run and play on his own without any supervision. He got to swim in the canal any time he wanted to.

Oliver didn't understand why Bart got to play in the water and have all that fun but he had to be on a leash and supervised whenever they got close to the canal.

That made Oliver mad.

One morning,
   Bart came up to Oliver
      while he was on a tie-out beside the camper and asked him
      to come swimming with him. Oliver was still mad at his mom
      so he slipped out of his collar and ran off with Bart
      to have fun in the canal.

Surely nothing bad
would happen.
His mom didn't
understand that a
dog just has to swim...
unless you are Rosie.

Bart and Oliver were having fun swimming and splashing around in the canal. Oliver saw some frogs and a turtle or two and then he saw this funny little lizard.

It was something Oliver hadn't ever seen before in the creek back home. It had lots and lots of little teeth but it was much smaller than him so he wasn't afraid of it at all.

All of a sudden Oliver heard a lot of splashing out in the middle of the canal. He saw Bart playing with another one of those lizards, but this one was MUCH,

MUCH, BIGGER!

That's when he realized Bart wasn't playing at all. He was frantically trying to get away from the alligator.

Luckily, Bart was a very fast swimmer. Both dogs scrambled out of the water and got to safety as fast as they could.

Oliver had never been so scared in all of his life and he had never been so glad to see his mom at that very moment.

She had been searching for him and, even though she was scared and upset with him for running away, she gave him a very big hug. She was so thankful he wasn't hurt.

While Oliver and his mom were walking back to their camper, they heard Bart whimpering and realized that he had been hurt by the alligator. His tail was bleeding and he had some other scratches and bumps on his face and legs.

Oliver's mom cleaned Bart's owies and patched him up, and then he went home to his family.

Oliver learned a very important lesson that day. He realized that his mom had been protecting him from danger when she wouldn't let him swim in the canal. It wasn't because she didn't want him to have fun.

He also started thinking that he owed Rosie an apology for making fun of her fear of water. What if an alligator had chased her too?

During the rest of the time Oliver and his mom were at the campground, he didn't get upset that he couldn't swim in the canal.

He had learned that he would have more fun running and playing in puddles with his pals.

He learned he could have just as much fun
wherever his mom took him...

...and that he would be safe to run and frolic
with his friends wherever he met them.

Tractor

Bear

Golf cart

Gnome

Sad dogs

Butterfly

Seek and Find

Oliver also likes to find things.
Can you help him find these objects
in the pages of this book?

Lady Bug

Snowman

Squirrel

Deer

Bunnies

Armadillo

Chipmunk

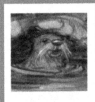

Otters

Dolphins

Crab

Shells

Palm trees

Turtles

Gator

Hawk

Seagull

Pelican

Bird nest

Robin

Egret

Oliver 2008-2019

Teri has spent most of her 25-plus year career
as a caricature artist and illustrator.

Over the years she has drawn caricatures from coast to
coast working at fairs and festivals.
Oliver accompanied her on many of these trips.

There have definitely been many walks and adventures
with friends...both 2 legged and 4 legged.

CPSIA information can be obtained
at www.ICGtesting.com
Printed in the USA
LVHW071201080222
710561LV00007B/259